ent:
Your child's l[obscured] here!

Every child learns to read in a different way and at his or her own speed. You can help your young reader improve and become more confident by encouraging his or her own interests and abilities. You can also guide your child's spiritual development by reading stories with biblical values and Bible stories, like I Can Read! books published by Zonderkidz. From books your child reads with you to the first books he or she reads alone, there are I Can Read! books for every stage of reading:

SHARED READING
Basic language, word repetition, and whimsical illustrations, ideal for sharing with your emergent reader.

1 **BEGINNING READING**
Short sentences, familiar words, and simple concepts for children eager to read on their own.

2 **READING WITH HELP**
Engaging stories, longer sentences, and language play for developing readers.

3 **READING ALONE**
Complex plots, challenging vocabulary, and high-interest topics for the independent reader.

4 **ADVANCED READING**
Short paragraphs, chapters, and exciting themes for the perfect bridge to chapter books.

I Can Read! books have introduced children to the joy of reading since 1957. Featuring award-winning authors and illustrators and a fabulous cast of beloved characters, I Can Read! books set the standard for

magical words **"I Can Read!"**

riching your child's reading experience.
Visit www.zonderkidz.com for more Zonderkidz I Can Read! titles.

Christ has accepted you. So accept one another in order to bring praise to God.
—*Romans 15:7*

Jake's New Friend

{story adapted from *Jonathan James Says "Let's Be Friends!"*
Chapter Three—The Picnic}

Requests for information should be addressed to:
Zonderkidz, Grand Rapids, Michigan 49530

Library of Congress Cataloging-in-Publication Data

Bowman, Crystal.
Jake's new friend / by Crystal Bowman ; illustrated by Karen Maizel.
p. cm. -- (Jake series) (I can read. Level 2)
"Story adapted from "Jonathan James says let's be friends!" chapter three,
The picnic"--T.p. verso.
ISBN 978-0-310-71678-5 (softcover)
[1. People with disabilities--Fiction. 2. Christian life--Fiction.] I. Maizel, Karen, ill. II.
Title.
PZ7.B68335Jan 2008
[E]--dc22

2008008377

Art Direction and Design: Jody Langley

Printed in China

08 09 10 • 4 3 2 1

I Can Read!™ READING 2 WITH HELP

Jake's New Friend

story by Crystal Bowman
pictures by Karen Maizel

It was Saturday.

Jake's family went to the park.

Jake liked to play at the park.

So did his little sister, Kelly.

Mother and Father brought food
for a picnic.
They saw another family at the park.

“We can have lunch with them,”

said Mother.

“Good idea,” said Father.

Mother and Father said hello
to the other family.
They were very nice.

They had a little girl named Liz.

Kelly wanted to play with her.

"Let's go swing," said Kelly.

"Okay," said Liz.

They also had a boy named Tom.

Tom sat in a chair with big wheels.

His legs were small.

He could not walk or run.

Jake did not want to play with Tom.

“Why don’t you play with Tom?”
Father asked Jake.
Jake looked down at the ground.
“I don’t want to,” he said.
“Tom cannot walk or run.
It wouldn’t be any fun.”

"God gave you strong legs,"

said Father.

"You can walk and run fast.

You can even climb trees.

But Tom can do other things.
Ask him what he likes to do."
Jake thought about what Father said.
"Okay, I'll talk to him," said Jake.

Jake went to talk to Tom.

Tom was playing with some blocks.

“What are you making?” asked Jake.

“I’m making a jet,” said Tom.

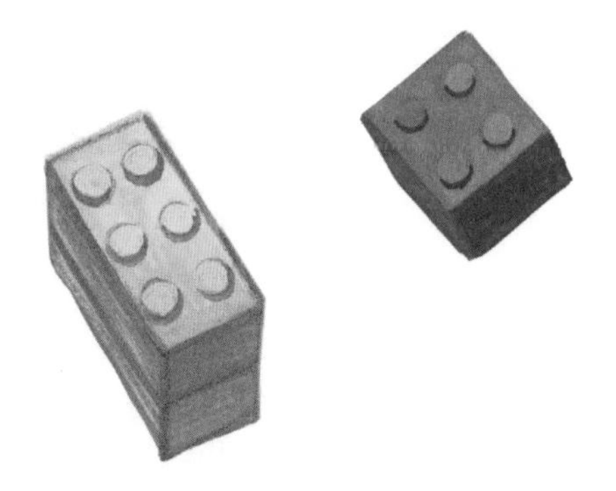

“Wow!” said Jake. “May I help?”

“Sure,” said Tom.

Jake helped Tom build a jet.

Soon it was finished.

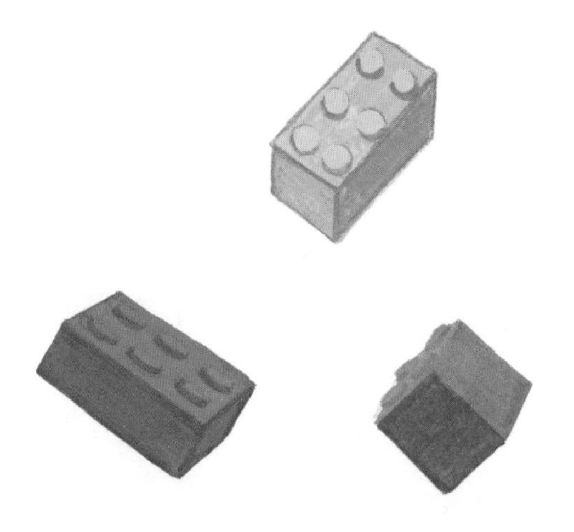

“What shall we do now?” asked Jake.

“Let’s have a race,” said Tom.

“We can race to the swings.”

“How can we race?” asked Jake.

“I will show you,” said Tom.

"When I push this button,
my chair goes fast," said Tom.

Jake got ready to race.

"One, two, three, go!" said Jake.

Tom pushed the button on his chair.

Jake ran next to Tom.

Then Tom got ahead of him.

"I won!" said Tom.

Jake was all out of breath.

“Let’s ride on the merry-go-round,”

said Tom.

“Can you help me get on?”

“Sure,” said Jake.

Jake helped Tom out of his chair.

Tom sat on the merry-go-round.

Jake gave it a push and hopped on.

They went around and around

until they were dizzy.

“Time for lunch,” called Mother.

Jake helped Tom get into his chair.

“I’ll race you back!” said Tom.

“One, two, three, go!”

Jake ran as fast as he could.

But Tom won again.

“I won!” said Tom.

“You always win!” said Jake.

Jake and Tom shared their lunch.

They had jelly sandwiches and juice.

After lunch it was time to go home.

“Good-bye, Tom,” said Jake.

“Good-bye,” said Tom.

“Maybe we can play again sometime.”

“I would like that,” said Jake.

“We can make another jet.

We can ride the merry-go-round.

And we can have more races.”

“Maybe I will let you win,” said Tom.

Jake gave Tom a high five.

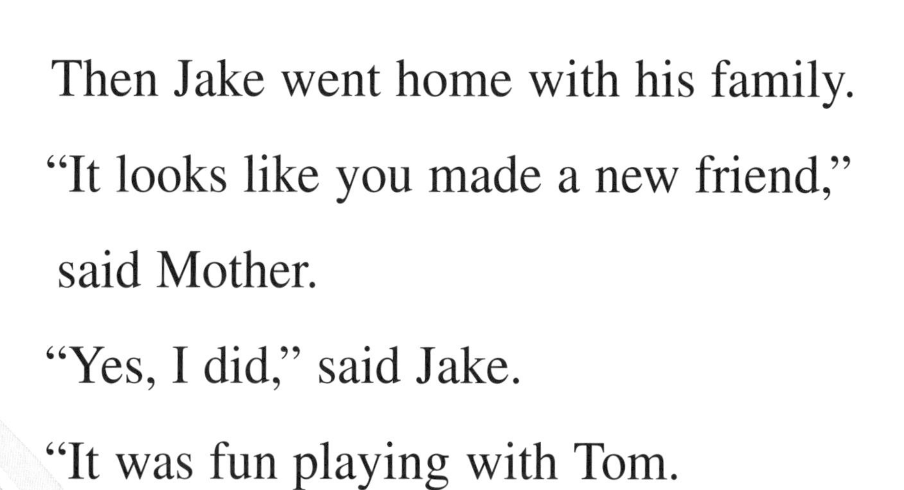

Then Jake went home with his family.

"It looks like you made a new friend," said Mother.

"Yes, I did," said Jake.

"It was fun playing with Tom.

We like to do the same things."

Jake was glad he went to the park.
He was happy that he could run.
And he was happy that God
gave him a new friend.